100 Things

you should know about

Myths &
Legends

100 Things
you should know about
Myths &
Legends

Fiona Macdonald

Consultant: Rupert Matthews

MASON CREST PUBLISHERS INC.
370 Reed Road
Broomall, Pennsylvania 19008
(866)MCP-BOOK (toll free)
www.masoncrest.com

ISBN: 978-1-4222-2002-3
Series ISBN (15 titles): 978-1-4222-1993-5

First Printing
9 8 7 6 5 4 3 2 1

Cataloging-in-Publication Data on file with the Library of Congress.
Printed in the U.S.A.

First published in 2009 by Miles Kelly Publishing Ltd
Bardfield Centre, Great Bardfield, Essex, CM7 4SL

Editorial Director: Belinda Gallagher

Art Director: Jo Brewer

Assistant Editor: Sarah Parkin

Editorial Assistant: Claire Philip

Volume Designers: Julia Harris, Simon Lee

Image Manager: Lorraine King

Indexer: Jane Parker

Production Manager: Elizabeth Brunwin

Reprographics: Stephan Davis, Jennifer Hunt, Ian Paulyn

ACKNOWLEDGEMENTS
The publishers would like to thank the following artists
who have contributed to this book:

Mike Foster, Ian Jackson, Patricia Ludlow,
Andrea Morandi, Mike Saunders, Mike White
Cover artwork: Ian Jackson

All other artwork from the Miles Kelly Artwork Bank

The publishers would like to thank the following
sources for the use of their photographs:

Page 2–3 2005 TopFoto/Warner Bro/TopFoto.co.uk; 6–7 TopFoto.co.uk; 8 Javarman/Fotolia.com; 12 Bettmann/Corbis;
14 Snap/Rex Features; 17 Everett Collection/Rex Features; 21 Bettmann/Corbis; 22 Everett Collection/Rex Features;
29 Everett Collection/Rex Features; 30 Photolibrary; 31 Phillipe Lissac/Godong/Corbis; 33 The Gallery Collection/Corbis;
35 NMeM/Science & Society; 37 Everett Collection/Rex Features; 40 Snap/Rex Features;
41(t) Warner Br/Everett/Rex Features, (b) Photos 12/Alamy; 42 Tim Rooke/Rex Features; 43(t) Snap/Rex Features,
(b) Julia Bayne/Robert Harding/Rex Features; 44(t) Christopher Cormack/Corbis, (b) Matt Baron/BEI/Rex Features;
45 Columbia/Everett/Rex Features; 46(bl) Masatoshi Okauchi/Rex Features, (m) ImageState/Alamy

All other photographs are from:

Corel, digitalSTOCK, digitalvision, iStockphoto.com, John Foxx, PhotoAlto,
PhotoDisc, PhotoEssentials, PhotoPro, Stockbyte

Contents

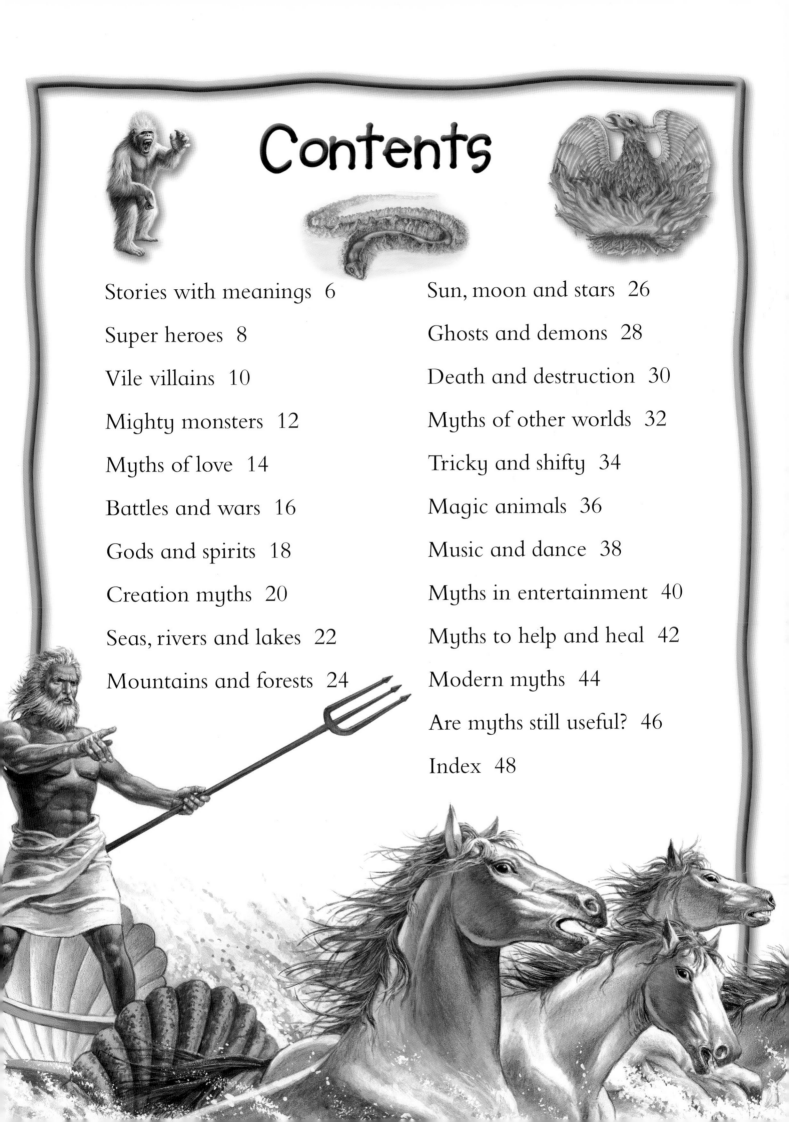

1 **Myths and legends are stories with meanings that have been enjoyed by people for thousands of years.** Myths explore beliefs and ideas or reveal truths about human nature. Legends are stories about one particular person, place, community or nation. Traditionally, myths and legends were passed on by word of mouth, but today they are told in books, films and TV dramas, and they even inspire computer and video games.

◄ A scene from the film *The Lord of the Rings: The Fellowship of the Ring* (2001). Its story is based on themes from several north European myths and legends.

Super heroes

2 Heroes perform extraordinary actions to help other people or to gain glory. Legends about Britain's King Arthur tell how he fought invaders, battled monsters, entered the Underworld and led his knights in search of a magic cauldron called the Holy Grail. They claim that Arthur is not dead, but sleeping, and he will return when Britain is in danger.

▲ Legends tell how, when he was a boy, Arthur was able to pull a magic sword from a stone. This was a sign that one day he would be king.

3 Hercules was a Greek hero. Hera, queen of the gods, drove him insane and he murdered his wife and children. The king sent Hercules to perform Twelve Labors (mighty tasks). He braved man-eating birds, a wild boar and a ferocious lion.

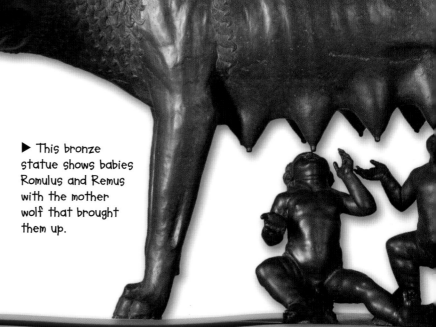

4 Many myths aim to explain the origins of important places. Twins Romulus and Remus were cared for by a mother wolf and they grew up to be brave warriors. They planned to build a new city, but argued. Romulus killed Remus and finished the city alone. It grew rich and powerful—and was named Rome after him.

► This bronze statue shows babies Romulus and Remus with the mother wolf that brought them up.

5 Botoque brought fire to the world. In Brazil, legends tell how he climbed up a cliff and met a jaguar carrying a bow and arrows and dead wild animals. The jaguar took Botoque to its home and cooked its catch over a fire. One day, the jaguar's wife quarrelled with Botoque. Angry and afraid, he climbed back down the cliff to the human world—and took the jaguar's fire with him.

6 Hindu Prince Arjuna won a bride because of his skill with a bow and arrows. When the king held a competition to find a husband for his daughter, Arjuna decided to enter. The target looked impossible—a model fish, swinging on a rope, reflected in a pool of water. However, Arjuna shot the fish in the eye and won.

▶ Disguised as a black carrion crow, the Celtic war goddess Babdh ("Fury"), hovers over mythical hero Cuchulainn as he fights his last, fatal battle.

7 Ireland's hero, Cuchulainn, was more than merely mortal. From childhood, he was stronger than other boys, and as a young man he was trained by a warrior witch in Scotland. In battle, he became a bloodthirsty monster—an eerie light glowed around him and his howling drove enemies mad with fear. In his final battle, Cuchulainn had his friends tie him to an ancient standing stone so that he could die fighting.

Vile villains

▶ According to Chinese myths, the gods locked Sun Wukong inside a mountain for 500 years to punish him for stealing the Peaches of Immortality.

8 Sun Wukong, the Chinese Monkey King, was a menace. He caused so much mischief on Earth and in hell that the gods took him up to heaven. He was sent to work in a garden where a miraculous peach tree grew— its fruits gave immortality. Sun Wukong ate them all and escaped back to Earth.

9 Some villains kill the things they love. One day, a nobleman called Bluebeard left his wife alone and told her not to unlock one of the doors in the castle. She was curious and opened it. Inside, she found Bluebeard's earlier wives—all had been murdered. When Bluebeard returned, he prepared to kill his new wife too. She was rescued by her brothers just in time.

PEACH MELBA

You will need:

a peach   ten raspberries
ice-cream or frozen yogurt

1. Cut the peach in half.
Remove the skin and pit.
2. Put each peach half, cut side
up, on a plate.
3. Add ice-cream or frozen
yogurt on each peach half.
4. Put a few raspberries on top
and the others round the side.

12 Ancient Egyptian legends tell of evil
dragon Apep, the Lord of Darkness. He
attacked the sun god every night on his journey
through the Underworld. However, armies of
dead souls always fought against Apep and
defeated him. So the sun god sailed safely on,
ready to rise and shine again in the morning.

10 The Morrigan (Ghost Queen)
was a goddess of love and death in
myths from Ireland. She could change
from a gentle girl to an old woman, a
slippery eel, a fierce wolf or a
bloodthirsty crow. The Morrigan could
cast spells and see into the future. She
warned her friends of danger, but
terrified enemies with the news that
their death was approaching.

▶ The ancient Egyptian myth of Apep the dragon was a
magical way of explaining what happened to the sun each
night between sunset and sunrise.

11 Kintu was a hunter from Uganda,
Africa. He climbed up into the sky to marry
Nambi, the High God's daughter. The High
God warned Kintu to take Nambi to Earth
before Death asked to go with them.
However, Nambi forgot something and
went back to the sky. When she returned
to Earth, Death came with her.

Mighty monsters

13 Huge and powerful, it's never safe to meddle with a monster. Some are good and some are bad, but all are dangerous! In Greek myths, the Hydra was a huge snake. Its fangs dripped poison, and its coils crushed victims. Greek hero Hercules was sent to kill it, but each time he cut off its head, two more grew to replace it.

▲ Hercules fights the Hydra. He only managed to defeat it after his nephew, Iolaus, came to help. He burnt the Hydra's necks with fire before new heads could grow.

▲ Mystery picture! No one (except the person who took it) knows for sure whether this photo of Bigfoot is genuine or a fake.

14 For hundreds of years in North America, people have reported sightings of a huge, ape-like creature living in the forests. They have given it many names, such as Bigfoot, the Sasquatch or the Wendigo. In 1967, two men claimed to have filmed Bigfoot at Bluff Creek, California. No one knows if the film was genuine.

15 The ancient Egyptians believed that after death a person's heart was weighed against the Feather of Truth. This showed whether or not they had led good, honest lives. If a heart failed the test, it was gobbled up by the monster Ammut—part lion, part hippo and part crocodile.

16 Around 1500, explorers in South America heard legends of El Dorado (the Golden One)—a man or monster made of gold. They searched everywhere but never found him. El Dorado was actually a new king, covered in gold dust during a special ritual to mark the start of his reign.

17 Malaveyovo was a giant cannibal who lived in Papua New Guinea. He raged around the island devouring men, women and children. The surviving islanders decided to give their best fruit and vegetables to Malaveyovo. If he ate them all, he would feel too full to go on eating humans!

▶ Grendel's mother crawls out of the swamp ready to avenge the death of her monster son.

18 Anglo-Saxon legends tell how Grendel, a man-eating monster, lurked in swampy fens. The warrior Beowulf killed Grendel with his bare hands. Then Grendel's grisly mother came to avenge her son's death, and Beowulf seemed doomed to die. However, he saved himself with a magic sword.

Myths of love

19 The story of Beauty and the Beast was written around 500 years ago. When Beauty was sent to live with the Beast she was frightened, but the Beast was kind and good and she fell in love with him. The Beast asked Beauty to marry him and she agreed. This broke a wicked spell that had changed the Beast's shape and he turned back into a young man.

▼ In this scene from the classic French film, *La Belle et la Bête* (*Beauty and the Beast*, 1946), a kiss breaks the spell that has turned a young man into a monster.

◄ The Irish myth *Deirdre of the Sorrows* tells how jealous love can lead to tragedy.

20 Wise men warned that Deirdre would bring suffering to Ireland. The king locked her in a castle out of harm's way, but he fell in love with her. Deirdre already loved Naoise, a young warrior, but the king, angry and jealous, had him murdered. Deirdre was heartbroken and killed herself. The king was slain by his own soldiers, appalled at his cruelty.

21 Khori Tumed was walking by Lake Baikal in Siberia when nine swans swooped down, took off their feathers and turned into young women. Khori Tumed hid one set of feathers so that one swan-woman could not fly. She married him and they had eleven sons. Years later, she asked Khori Tumed for her feathers. She put them on, soared up to the sky and flew away forever.

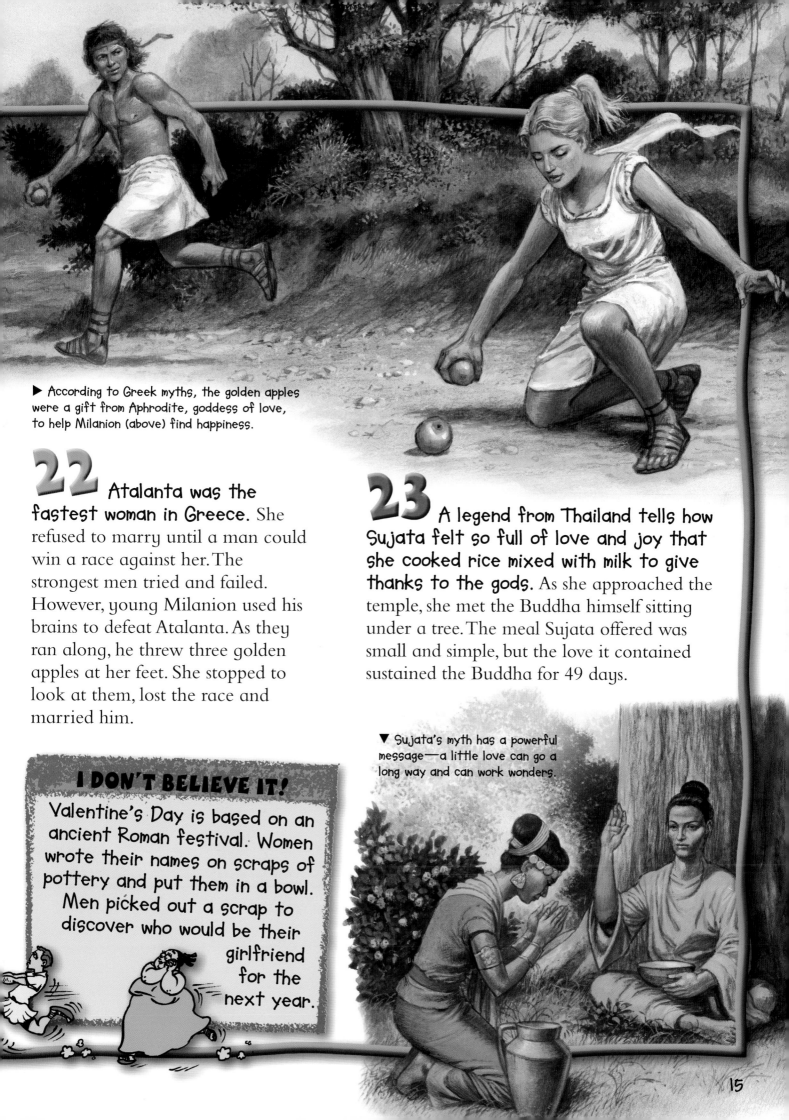

▶ According to Greek myths, the golden apples were a gift from Aphrodite, goddess of love, to help Milanion (above) find happiness.

22 Atalanta was the fastest woman in Greece. She refused to marry until a man could win a race against her. The strongest men tried and failed. However, young Milanion used his brains to defeat Atalanta. As they ran along, he threw three golden apples at her feet. She stopped to look at them, lost the race and married him.

23 A legend from Thailand tells how Sujata felt so full of love and joy that she cooked rice mixed with milk to give thanks to the gods. As she approached the temple, she met the Buddha himself sitting under a tree. The meal Sujata offered was small and simple, but the love it contained sustained the Buddha for 49 days.

▼ Sujata's myth has a powerful message—a little love can go a long way and can work wonders.

I DON'T BELIEVE IT!

Valentine's Day is based on an ancient Roman festival. Women wrote their names on scraps of pottery and put them in a bowl. Men picked out a scrap to discover who would be their girlfriend for the next year.

15

Battles and wars

24 Many myths feature famous fighters, such as Gilgamesh, king of Sumer (now Iraq), and Enkidu, a ruffian from the desert. Together they had many adventures. They fought Humbaba, the giant who guarded the forests, then killed the Bull of Heaven, who had caused great destruction.

▲ Gilgamesh raises his axe, ready to strike the giant Humbaba. Many ancient myths link tall, strong trees with giant, supernatural creatures.

25 According to myths from New Zealand, the first fish lived in trees. A violent storm drove them from the trees into the water. This made Tane, god of the trees, jealous of the sea god, Tangaroa. They fought and their quarrel still continues—the stormy sea tries to flood the land and boats made from timber try to conquer the waves.

26 The valkyries were nine warrior goddesses who served the Viking god Odin. They rode on flying horses and galloped across battlefields. The valkyries decided which warriors should live or die and they carried dead heroes to Valhalla (Warriors' Hall) to feast forever.

▶ Valkyries were warriors, but also wise teachers. Myths told how they taught young warriors to fight well and win battles.

► In this scene from the 1999 epic film, *The Messenger: The Story of Joan of Arc*, Joan leads French armies to victory against English invaders.

27 The Mahabharata (written down around 100 BCE) is the longest epic poem in the world. It tells ancient Indian legends about heroes and villains, gods and demons. It ends with the battle of Kurukshetra that brings peace to the kingdoms of India – but only after terrible slaughter and suffering. The poem asks important questions such as "Is war good or bad?"

28 Joan of Arc, a farmer's daughter from France, believed she was guided by heavenly voices. Aged just 17, she led French soldiers to victory against the English at the Battle of Orléans in 1429. She was captured, put on trial for breaking religious laws and executed in 1431. Today, Joan is remembered as a heroine who saved France.

29 In 1914, during World War 1, a troop of British soldiers were in deadly danger. In the sky overhead, they thought they saw St. George and an army of angels guarding them and guiding them to safety. Whether this vision is true or not, the men all reached the British camp alive.

Gods and spirits

30 Many myths and legends tell of gods and spirits that live in wild, remote places. Poseidon, god of the sea, whipped up wild waves and blasted the land with earthquakes and thunder.

▶ This wood-and-feather mask portrays Tarqeq, the Moon Spirit. It was worn by dancers performing scenes from Inuit myths and legends.

31 In myths from icy Arctic regions, Tarqeq, the Moon Spirit, looks down from the sky. Mostly he is kind and helps hunters find animals to catch for their food. However, when he is angry he sends bad weather, bad hunting and bad health to all.

◀ Greek god Poseidon carries a golden trident (three-pronged spear) as he drives his horses across the waves.

▶ One of the symbols of Tlaloc is a double-headed serpent.

32 According to Aztec myths, Tlaloc, the rain god, ruled over a green, fertile kingdom high in the mountains. Usually it was hidden in the clouds—only Tlaloc's victims, people who had drowned or been killed by lightning, could enter. Living people worshipped Tlaloc as a kind god and as a killer. He sent rain that helped crops grow, but also savage storms that destroyed them.

33 The Celtic peoples of Britain worshipped many nature spirits, such as Sulis, a healing goddess who lived in hot springs in southwest England. When the Romans invaded Britain in 54 CE, they built a temple over the springs to honor Minerva, goddess of wisdom. The springs and parts of the temple survive today in the city of Bath.

34 Followers of Shinto, the ancient religion of Japan, believe that everything in nature has its own invisible kami (spirit). A kami can be kind or evil. The kami that control the waves, weather and volcanoes were especially honored and feared by Japanese people.

▲ This Roman temple at Bath honors a legendary Celtic water goddess.

35 Traditional tales from Australia describe the Namodoro—scary, slithery spirits made of skin and bone. They swish through the sky like shooting stars, then swoop down to snatch the old and ill with their long, sharp claws.

Creation myths

36 Jewish, Christian and Muslim holy writings record an ancient belief—God made Adam, the first man, and Eve, the first woman. He gave them Paradise as their home but told them they must not eat the fruit of the Tree of Knowledge. However, a snake persuaded Eve to taste the fruit and Adam copied her. God sent them out of Paradise to punish them.

◄ Myths tell how beautiful apples grew on the Tree of Knowledge, found only in Paradise.

QUIZ

1. Who was the first man and the first woman?
2. Who did Mwetsi, the full Moon, marry?
3. How many times did the Aztecs believe that the world had been created and destroyed before?

Answers:
1. Adam and Eve 2. Morning Star and Evening Star 3. Four times

37 Mwetsi, the full Moon, went to live in Zimbabwe, Africa. He married Morning Star and Evening Star. Evening Star bore killers—lions, leopards, snakes and scorpions. One of the snakes bit Mwetsi and he grew thin and feeble—everything in his kingdom fell sick or hungry. To bring back life and health, Mwetsi's children killed him and chose a strong new ruler.

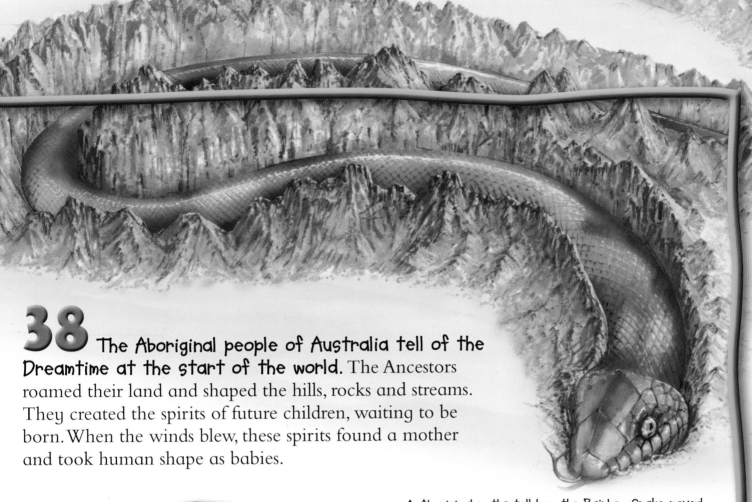

38 The Aboriginal people of Australia tell of the Dreamtime at the start of the world. The Ancestors roamed their land and shaped the hills, rocks and streams. They created the spirits of future children, waiting to be born. When the winds blew, these spirits found a mother and took human shape as babies.

▲ Aboriginal myths tell how the Rainbow Snake moved over the Earth, leaving valleys and hills in its wake.

▲ This huge sun stone is carved with glyphs (picture symbols) recording Aztec myths about creation. In the center is the Sun of Fire.

39 After the great flood at the beginning of the world, Chinese goddess Nu Gua was lonely—there were no people. Nu Gua took some mud and shaped the first man and woman. Then she dipped a branch in water and scattered drops far and wide. Each drop became a new person.

40 Aztecs believed that the world had been created and destroyed four times before. Each world had been ruled by a different sun. The first was the Sun of Air, second was the Sun of Wind, third the Sun of Rain and fourth the Sun of Water. The Aztecs' own sun was the Sun of Fire.

Seas, rivers and lakes

41 In Greek legends, monsters Scylla and Charybdis lay in wait to wreck ships. Charybdis was a huge whirlpool that sucked sailors down to their death. Scylla was a six-headed monster, surrounded by sharp rocks. They destroyed any ships that sailed too close to them.

Scylla

▼ This photo of a mysterious shape rising from the waters of Loch Ness was taken in 1934. Does it show a seal, a shadow, part of a dead tree, a wrecked boat—or a monster?

42 Loch Ness, in northern Scotland, is the largest lake in Britain. For over 1,000 years, legends have reported that a mysterious creature lives there. Since 1933, many investigators have claimed to have seen or photgraphed it. But no reliable evidence has ever been found to prove "Nessie's" existence.

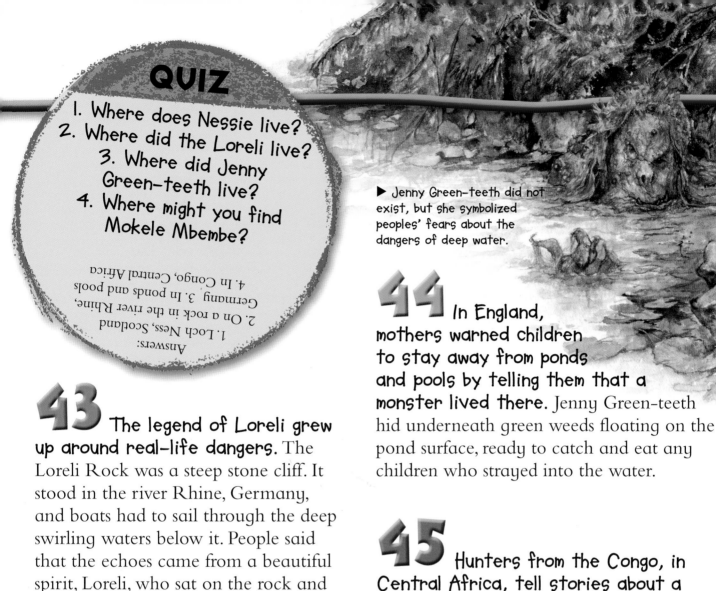

▶ Jenny Green-teeth did not exist, but she symbolized peoples' fears about the dangers of deep water.

44 **In England, mothers warned children to stay away from ponds and pools by telling them that a monster lived there.** Jenny Green-teeth hid underneath green weeds floating on the pond surface, ready to catch and eat any children who strayed into the water.

43 **The legend of Loreli grew up around real-life dangers.** The Loreli Rock was a steep stone cliff. It stood in the river Rhine, Germany, and boats had to sail through the deep swirling waters below it. People said that the echoes came from a beautiful spirit, Loreli, who sat on the rock and called sailors toward her—to die.

45 **Hunters from the Congo, in Central Africa, tell stories about a legendary creature called Mokele Mbembe that lives in the forests.** It is huge, has a heavy body, a long neck and a tiny head. No one knows if it exists or if it is just imaginary.

▼ Greek monster Charybdis was a legend based on fact. There really was a dangerous whirlpool off the island of Sicily (now part of Italy).

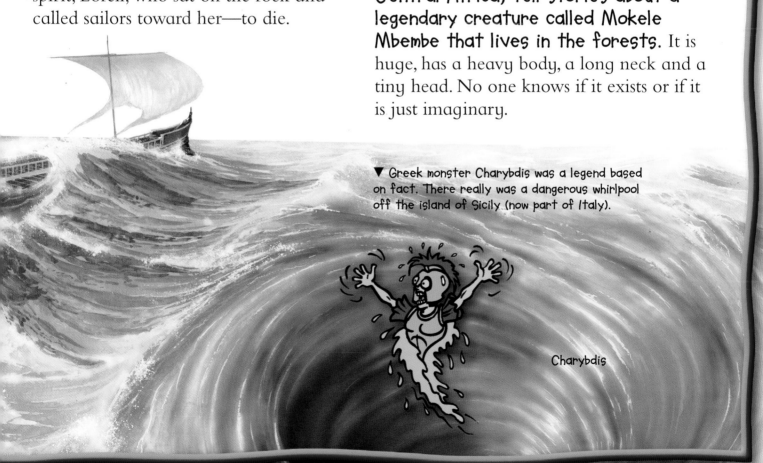

Charybdis

Mountains and forests

▶ Scientists know that a huge prehistoric ape, *Gigantopithecus*, once lived in the jungles of northern India. The mythical Yeti might be a close relative.

46 High mountains, like the Himalayas in Asia, lie beyond the limits of human civilization. Many myths and legends portray them as refuges for mysterious creatures such as Yetis—shy, wild, hairy ape-men. Until recently, there was no proof that Yetis exist, but scientists are examining mysterious hairs brought back by travelers. They hope to find Yeti DNA in them.

47 **Like mountains, forests could be threatening.** No one knew what lurked among the shadows. In ancient Britain, people thought that the magical and mysterious Green Man lived among the trees. He was tall and strong like a tree trunk and had leaves growing in his hair.

◀ The Green Man is a symbol of death, decay and rebirth. Legends about woodland hero Robin Hood may be based on him.

49 **Russian myths warned of Nightingale the Bandit who lay in wait to trap travelers.** Half-man, half-bird, he lived high in the trees. He howled, whistled and screamed to conjure up a wicked wind that killed everything.

48 **Ancient Greek stories told of the nine Muses, beautiful young goddesses who ruled over the creative arts.** They lived on Mount Parnassus, one of the highest mountains in Greece. Today, our words "music" and "museum" are based on their name.

50 **Some myths and legends describe the power of nature.** In Indonesia, the Dayak people told stories about Pulang Gana, a rainforest spirit. When the first Dayak cut down trees to make fields and plant crops, Pulang Gana made the trees grow back. He made a bargain that he would let the farmers have their fields in return for offerings.

Sun, moon and stars

51 The sun, moon and stars have been far beyond human reach for most of history. However, many myths and legends tell of journeys toward them. Using wax and feathers, Greek inventor Daedalus made wings for himself and Icarus, his son. Icarus soared too high. The sun melted the wax in his wings and he fell into the sea.

▶ Icarus falls from the sky as the wax melts on his wings. His myth may be a warning not to explore too far, or just good advice to be careful.

▼ A leaping rabbit is one of the creatures that can be spotted on the moon.

52 Many people have thought that the moon has a human face. Others have imagined different creatures on its shining surface. The Anglo-Saxons thought they saw Eastre, goddess of spring and the dawn, who took the shape of a hare. Today, Eastre's hare has been turned into the Easter Bunny—everyone has forgotten its link with the moon.

53 Aztec god-king Quetzalcoatl was a feathered snake, the god of wind and a high priest. He ruled wisely but his people turned away from him to serve his cruel twin brother, the god of war. To bring peace, Quetzalcoatl sacrificed himself on a blazing fire. His heart was carried to the sky and became the Morning Star.

▲ This picture from an Aztec Codex (folding picture book) portrays the god Quetzalcoatl. He carries a magic feathered shield in one hand. A hummingbird, one of his sacred symbols, hovers close by.

54 Myths from North America tell how light came to the world. In the beginning, everything was dark. Grandmother Spider shaped a little bowl from clay and climbed up to the sun. She took a tiny piece of light, dropped it into the bowl and scuttled quickly home. Even today, spiders' webs are shaped like the sun's rays.

55 Kui Xing was very clever— and very ugly. He won top prize in China's toughest exams, but the Emperor refused to look at him or reward him. Kui Xing rushed to a cliff to hurl himself into the sea, but a monster, half-turtle, half-fish, leapt from the waves to save him. It carried Kui Xing to the sky, where he lives among the stars and shares their sparkling beauty.

QUIZ

1. Who tried to fly to the sun?
2. What is one of the creatures spotted on the moon?
3. Who took light from the sun?
4. Who went to live with the stars?

Answers:
1. Daedalus and Icarus
2. A leaping rabbit
3. Grandmother Spider
4. Kui Xing

56 The ghost of the *Flying Dutchman* features in stories about the sea. According to legend, this ship haunts the Cape of Good Hope at the southern tip of Africa. Its proud captain ignored storm warnings and sailed on through wild winds and waves. A vision appeared on deck and begged him to turn back. However, the *Flying Dutchman*'s captain refused and his ship was wrecked.

▶ Sailors said that seeing the ghostly *Flying Dutchman* meant that death or disaster would soon follow. Scientists suggest that the mysterious ghost ship is probably a mirage.

I DON'T BELIEVE IT!

Magician Simon Magus (died 60 CE) claimed to be able to fly. He demanded to be buried in a deep trench and promised that his ghost would soon come back to haunt the living. So far, no one has seen it!

57 Caribbean myths describe zombies—the bodies of dead people brought back to life in secret Voodoo ceremonies. The myths say that zombies will do anything, good or bad, for the Voodoo magician who revived them.

58 Myths from ancient Arabia described ghostly djinn (genies). They could change into countless shapes but most often appeared as snakes, dogs and humans. Djinn tempted travelers away from safe tracks to get lost in the desert. In the *Thousand and One Nights* collection of Middle Eastern myths and legends, a djinni (genie) helps the young hero Aladdin.

▲ In traditional stories from the Middle East, Aladdin could call a mighty djinni (genie) to help him by polishing a small metal lamp.

59 In China, myths suggest how silk was discovered. While her father was away, Can Nu said, "I'd marry anyone who found Father!" The farm horse heard this, galloped off and returned with her father. Frightened by Can Nu's promise, he shot the horse and skinned it. The dried skin—now a ghost— wrapped itself around Can Nu and carried her into a tree. There she turned into a worm and her mournful words became silk thread.

60 Blood-sucking vampires appear in legends from many different lands. They are dead people who cannot find peaceful rest. They have pale skin, blood-red lips, long, sharp fingernails and fangs. They cannot stand daylight and they need to drink blood from living victims. Anyone they bite becomes a vampire. The most famous vampire is Count Dracula.

▶ Count Dracula, portrayed by Christopher Lee, bares his fangs in the horror movie *Dracula* (1958). The story of Dracula was based on traditional myths and legends from eastern Europe.

61 Who decides how long we will live?
Many myths try to answer this question.
The ancient Greeks believed in three
powerful goddesses called the Fates.
Clotho, the Spinner, spun the thread
of each person's life, Lachesis, the
Giver, measured its length and Atropos,
the Inescapable, cut the thread
when it was time to die.

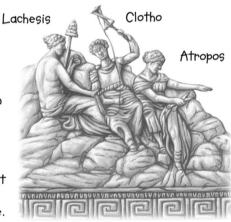

Lachesis   Clotho   Atropos

▶ The three Fates
controlled the length
of all life on Earth.
They were only
challenged once, by
Asclepius, god of
medicine, who brought
one of his dead
patients back to life.

◀ The mythical Grim Reaper is a mixture of the Greek
harvest god Kronos and the ancient Jewish Angel of
Death. He is sometimes kindly, sometimes frightening.

62 In farming countries, especially in
Europe and North America, death was often
portrayed as a skeleton reaper (harvester).
He carried a scythe (a curved, long-handled
blade). Traditionally, scythes were used to cut
down grass while it was tall and healthy. This
image of death may have been inspired by words
in the Bible—"All flesh is as grass…"

I DON'T BELIEVE IT!

Greek people were afraid of
the Fates and did not want
to offend or encourage them.
They didn't like to use the
Fates' real names
so they called
them "The Kindly
Ones."

63 **Kali is the terrifying Hindu goddess of Death.** Myths describe how she fought countless demons and got so drunk with killing that she almost destroyed the world. Kali is usually shown dancing through time and space wearing a necklace of human heads.

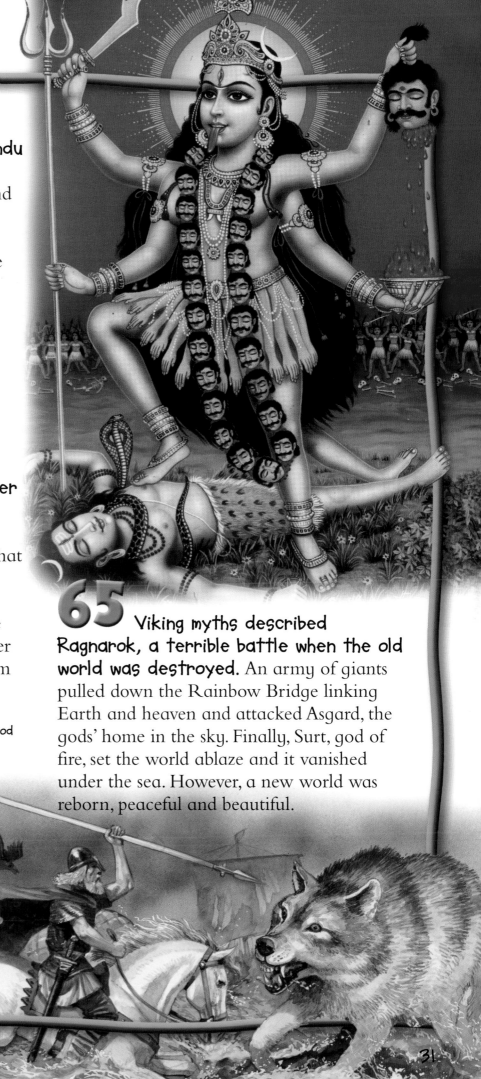

► The Hindu goddess Kali, dancing on a demon she has defeated.

64 **The legend of Faust is based on a real person, astrologer Dr. Johann Faustus, who lived in Germany around 1500 CE.** While Faust was alive, there were rumors that he used magic to learn secret skills. After he died, people said that Faust had sold his soul in return for all the world's knowledge and pleasure. After 24 years, the Devil came to drag him down to Hell.

▼ Viking myths told how, at Ragnarok, the wise god Odin was devoured by a monster wolf, and Thor, god of Thunder, was killed by a giant serpent.

65 **Viking myths described Ragnarok, a terrible battle when the old world was destroyed.** An army of giants pulled down the Rainbow Bridge linking Earth and heaven and attacked Asgard, the gods' home in the sky. Finally, Surt, god of fire, set the world ablaze and it vanished under the sea. However, a new world was reborn, peaceful and beautiful.

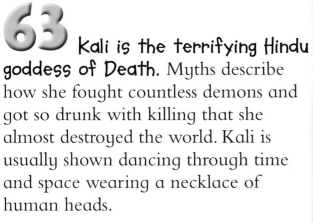

Myths of other worlds

66 Many myths and legends suggest that there is an Afterlife or an Underworld where dead souls survive. The ancient Romans believed that the entrance to Hades (the Underworld) was guarded by Cerberus, a giant dog with three heads, which ate anyone who tried to escape.

67 Among the Celtic peoples of Europe, myths described a country known as Tir nan Og (Land of Youth). There was no pain, decay or suffering—all was beauty and delight. The living might visit Tir nan Og, but they rarely returned to the ordinary world. If they did return, they found that hundreds of years had passed and that they were all alone, among strangers.

▲ The Celtic paradise of Tir nan Og was a beautiful land without old age, illness or death.

▲ Fierce Cerberus was friendly and gentle only once— when Greek hero Orpheus played music.

▼ Ancient Egyptians prayed to Isis for help in this world and everlasting life in the kingdom of the dead.

68 Isis, the mightiest, most mysterious goddess in Egypt, was a devoted wife and mother. She used her powers to bring Osiris, her dead husband, home from the kingdom of the dead. Osiris had been cut into pieces by his wicked brother. Isis put him back together and breathed new life into him by fanning him gently with her wings.

DESIGN A GARDEN

The idea of Paradise has inspired many artists and gardeners in Muslim lands. Design a Paradise Garden with trees, flowers and fountains. Look at pictures of Muslim gardens in library books or on the Internet for ideas.

▶ In this picture, painted in Christian Europe around 1500 CE, Adam and Eve are shown (at bottom of page) being chased out of Paradise by an angel with a sword.

69 Originally, "Paradise" was a Persian (Iranian) word that meant "beautiful walled garden." For many centuries it has been used by Muslims and Christians as another name for Heaven. Religious stories describe it as a place of peace and joy, with flowers, trees, pools and fountains.

70 The land of Huarochiri once was alive with birds, the fields gave generous crops and the dead came back to life. Surrounded by pleasure, the people grew lazy. As punishment, their god Pariacaca sent them to a cold, dry and stony new land. This legend from South America may be linked to real events, when invaders drove the Huarochiri people out of their homeland.

Tricky and shifty

71 According to legend, Eshu was the greatest trickster in West Africa. He delighted in chaos and confusion. Eshu would wait at crossroads and send travelers in the wrong direction or visit markets to make traders argue. He persuaded the sun and moon to change places—turning day into night.

▶ This wooden staff from Africa is topped with a carving of Eshu. In the past, it would have been carried by important people or used in traditional ceremonies.

▼ Traditional carvings from Canada often portray mythical creatures, such as Raven the trickster, together with images of ancestors and heroes.

72 In Canadian myths, Raven was a trickster. One day, on a beach, he met a woman with eight long braids. He mocked her hairstyle—she grew angry, but he continued. She changed into an octopus, pinned him to a boulder and said, "unless you mend your manners, I'll keep you here to drown!" The trickster was tricked!

▶ This fake photo, created in 1917, claims to show tiny fairies dancing while a young girl watches.

73

Fairies, ghosts and spirits have the power to change their shape and to transform people. In a Scottish legend, Tam Lin was snatched away by the Fairy Queen. Janet, his human sweetheart, was determined not to let him go. The fairies changed Tam into water, a blazing fire and a roaring lion. Still Janet held him. At last, Tam changed back into his human shape and the fairies disappeared.

▶ Loki's shifty face peers from this Viking stone carving, made around 1,000 years ago.

74

Legends from China tell of fox fairies who can change their shape. Sometimes they appear as pretty young women and at other times they take the shape of old men. They can pass through solid rocks and walls, float in the air and survive under water.

75

Perhaps a god, perhaps a giant, Loki was weird and wonderful. Viking myths claim that he gave birth to a monster wolf and the poisonous World Serpent. He loved malice and mischief and he played a mean, murderous trick, killing the beautiful god Balder with a sprig of mistletoe. As a punishment, Loki was chained, but later he broke free to cause more trouble.

QUIZ

1. Who tricked Raven?
2. Who freed Tam Lin from the fairies?
3. Who can walk though walls?
4. Who gave birth to a monster wolf and the poisonous World Serpent?

Answers:
1. Octopus woman 2. Janet
3. Fox fairies 4. Loki

Magic animals

76 **The phoenix was a giant bird, said to live for 500 years.** When its time came to die, it built a nest of fragrant twigs, climbed on top and set itself on fire. It burned for three days, then was reborn in the fire— young, strong and beautiful.

▶ Legends about the phoenix originated in ancient Egypt, where big, beautiful birds were worshipped at a temple dedicated to the bright, burning sun.

77 **Chinese myths tell how dragons rule the seas and rivers and fly along rainbows to make thunder.** Each one carries a pearl—like a raindrop—in its throat. In springtime, Chinese villagers held special festivals to ask the dragons to send rain to their fields.

◀ The name "dragon" comes from ancient Greek words meaning "keen sighted." Dragons were famous as guardians of kings, countries and treasure.

78 Myths from the Middle East tell of giant bird-like monsters called **rocs.** They dropped huge boulders on ships to sink them, but they could also be helpful—one rescued Arabian hero Sinbad the Sailor from death in the desert.

▲ Once, Sinbad was trapped in a deep, inaccessible valley. He escaped by clinging to a giant roc as it flew by, hunting for food.

79 Men who are bewitched or use magic to turn into wolves at full moon are called werewolves. They have large appetites and roam the countryside at night, hunting or digging up dead bodies to eat. They can only be killed by a silver bullet that shines like the moon.

▶ A mild-mannered man turns into a savage wolf in this still from the 1981 movie *An American Werewolf in London.*

Music and dance

80 Orpheus was the world's greatest singer—his music could tame wild beasts and move mountains. Greek myths tell how he vowed to bring his dead wife Eurydice back from the Underworld. Playing and singing, he led her toward the light. However, when he looked back toward her just once, Eurydice faded away into the darkness forever.

81 Myths often demonstrate the healing powers of music and dance. In ancient Egypt, Re, the sun god, was deeply depressed. No one could cheer him. Then Hathor, goddess of love, shook a sistrum (magic bells) and danced in front of him. She was so charming and graceful that Re started to smile again.

▲ Orpheus is overcome by grief and horror as his wife, Eurydice, disappears.

◀ An ancient Egyptian banquet. In many cultures, dancing was a way of praising the gods. Joyful, energetic dances also symbolized the gods' powers to create and sustain life.

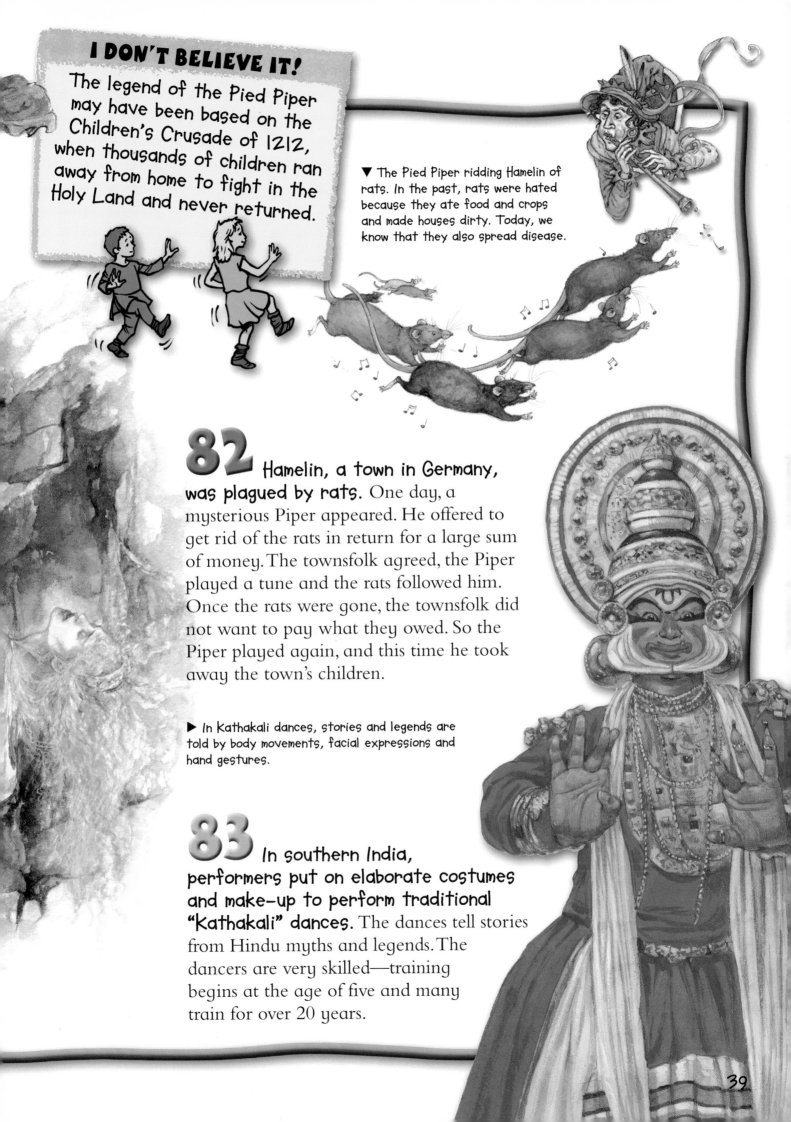

▼ The Pied Piper ridding Hamelin of rats. In the past, rats were hated because they ate food and crops and made houses dirty. Today, we know that they also spread disease.

82 Hamelin, a town in Germany, was plagued by rats. One day, a mysterious Piper appeared. He offered to get rid of the rats in return for a large sum of money. The townsfolk agreed, the Piper played a tune and the rats followed him. Once the rats were gone, the townsfolk did not want to pay what they owed. So the Piper played again, and this time he took away the town's children.

▶ In Kathakali dances, stories and legends are told by body movements, facial expressions and hand gestures.

83 In southern India, performers put on elaborate costumes and make-up to perform traditional "Kathakali" dances. The dances tell stories from Hindu myths and legends. The dancers are very skilled—training begins at the age of five and many train for over 20 years.

84 For over 600 years, the legendary adventures of Robin Hood have entertained audiences. From their hideout in Sherwood Forest, Robin and his men robbed weary travelers and waged war with the hated Sheriff of Nottingham. Although Robin was an outlaw and a thief, he refused to harm women and children and stole from the rich to give to the poor.

▶ Robin Hood gets ready to shoot an arrow from his longbow in this scene from the 1991 film *Robin Hood: Prince of Thieves*.

QUIZ

1. How old are the stories about Robin Hood?
2. When were heroes Batman and Superman created?
3. How old are Christmas pantomimes?

Answers:
1. About 600 years old
2. In the 1930s
3. Over 300 years old

86 Myths from Europe and Asia have inspired many of the greatest ballets, such as *Sleeping Beauty* and *Swan Lake*. All use music and dance to create dramatic scenes on stage, full of enchantment and delight. For over 300 years, myths have also inspired noisy, funny, Christmas shows called pantomimes.

▲ In this scene from *The Dark Knight* (2008), Batman soars through the air on an urgent mission to solve a terrible crime.

85 Superstar comic-book heroes Batman and Superman were created in the U.S. during the troubled times of the 1930s. Their amazing adventures brought pleasure to readers facing the threat of war. Like gods and heroes from ancient myths and legends, Batman and Superman are shape-shifters. They go on perilous quests, have supernatural powers and can fly.

87 Past myths and legends have inspired many of today's most popular books and films. *The Lord of the Rings, The Chronicles of Narnia* and the *Harry Potter* series all include heroes, villains, magic and monsters similar to those found in traditional tales.

◄ The film *The Chronicles of Narnia: The Lion, the Witch and the Wardrobe* (2005) features a beautiful, wicked White Witch who brings endless winter.

Myths to help and heal

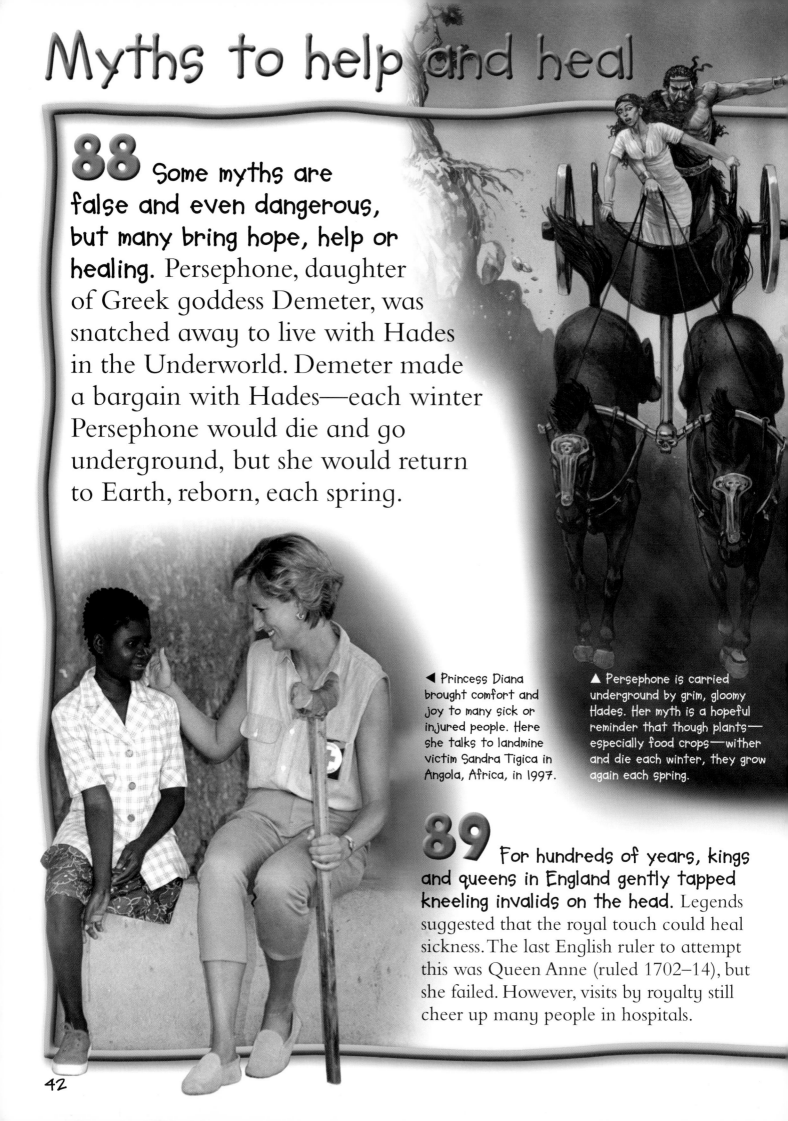

88 Some myths are false and even dangerous, but many bring hope, help or healing. Persephone, daughter of Greek goddess Demeter, was snatched away to live with Hades in the Underworld. Demeter made a bargain with Hades—each winter Persephone would die and go underground, but she would return to Earth, reborn, each spring.

◄ Princess Diana brought comfort and joy to many sick or injured people. Here she talks to landmine victim Sandra Tigica in Angola, Africa, in 1997.

▲ Persephone is carried underground by grim, gloomy Hades. Her myth is a hopeful reminder that though plants—especially food crops—wither and die each winter, they grow again each spring.

89 For hundreds of years, kings and queens in England gently tapped kneeling invalids on the head. Legends suggested that the royal touch could heal sickness. The last English ruler to attempt this was Queen Anne (ruled 1702–14), but she failed. However, visits by royalty still cheer up many people in hospitals.

▶ In this still from Walt Disney's 1940 cartoon film, Pinocchio's wooden nose has not only grown long, but has sprouted leaves as well!

90 In the Walt Disney cartoon film *Pinocchio*, Pinocchio's nose grows longer and longer each time he tells a lie. Disney based his film on an Italian children's story that was inspired by ancient traditional tales—they aimed to stop children telling lies. Disney made children laugh and perhaps this was a better way of encouraging them to be truthful.

91 In Ireland, people say that kissing the "Blarney Stone" (a huge rock in the wall of Blarney Castle) gives the gift of sweet-speaking. This cannot be proved, but perhaps the legend gives shy speakers extra confidence and makes their words flow more easily.

92 What happens to wasted time, broken promises, forgotten tasks, neglected duties and other things that we regret? In the past, people said that they ended up on the Moon. They stayed there forever to warn us to behave better and inspire us to lead good lives in the future.

▶ A tourist bends over backward to kiss the Blarney Stone. Many traditional myths say that success at difficult tasks brings great rewards.

KISSING THE BLARNEY STONE

TONGUE TWISTER

Practicing these tongue twisters might help you speak smoothly. Repeat as fast as you can:
Red truck, yellow truck.
Which witch wished wicked wishes?
Fighters fly frightfully fast.
Now try to invent a new tongue twister of your own.

Modern myths

93 Since the 1980s, mysterious "crop circle" patterns have appeared in fields throughout Europe and North America. They are made by crushing growing crops in geometric patterns. Modern "urban myths" have grown up to explain crop circles—for example, that they are made by aliens visiting Earth from outer space.

▲ Crop circles are probably made by practical jokers, but no one knows precisely how they manage to create them.

94 Many myths feature amazingly beautiful women and exceptionally handsome men. Today, the idea of perfect beauty lives on in the film and fashion industries. Few ordinary people look like supermodels or movie stars, but they like to gaze at "legendary" beauties on screen or in magazines.

◀ Movie star Angelina Jolie is famous not only for her beauty, but for campaigning to help disadvantaged children in many parts of the world. Here she is pictured with her partner Brad Pitt.

QUIZ

1. When did crop circles first appear?
2. In which country was Godzilla created?
3. What kind of wildlife inspired myths about mermaids?

Answers:
1. The 1980s 2. Japan 3. Dugongs

▶ Dugongs are about the same size and shape as plump human swimmers. It is easy to see how they once inspired myths about mermaids.

95
Giant lizard Godzilla is a modern mythical monster. Created in Japan in 1954, it has featured in many exciting films and manga cartoon books. Godzilla's enemies include other mythical creatures, such as evil robots and genetically engineered mutants.

▼ Like traditional monsters, Godzilla (right) can be terrifying, but he also uses his mighty powers to protect the Earth.

96
Science has explained some myths. In the past, sailors sighted beautiful mermaids, half-women, half-fish. Today, scientists think that these were dugongs, creatures related to whales and seals. Dugongs have fishy tails, but rounded heads, big eyes and a gentle expression. A female dugong holds her baby close under her flippers, just like a mother cradling a child.

Are myths still useful?

97 Over the past 200 years, science has explained many things that once seemed magical and mysterious. However, myths and legends have not disappeared. They still amuse or entertain us and appeal to our imagination. Scientific discoveries have inspired many new stories—some based on facts, some completely untrue.

▼ People have spotted flying saucers, sometimes called UFOs (Unidentified Flying Objects), for more than 60 years. Some people believe that they carry aliens from other planets.

◄ The brilliant skills and huge salaries of top soccer players such as Cristiano Ronaldo mean that they are often treated like larger-than-life legendary heroes.

98 Stories about famous people are immensely popular, even though many are exaggerated or untrue. What do these "celebrity myths" say about the people who read them? Are they looking for excitement, entertainment or a way of escaping for a while from their own everyday lives?

99 Myths still explain what we can't understand. In spite of modern safety precautions, ships are lost at sea every year. The reasons for these disasters are usually obvious, such as stormy weather. However, some wrecks remain mysterious and new legends try to explain them. In the "Bermuda Triangle" area of sea, close to the Caribbean, ships and planes are said to disappear for strange, supernatural reasons.

USA

BERMUDA

FLORIDA

BERMUDA TRIANGLE

ATLANTIC OCEAN

BAHAMAS

CUBA

DOMINICAN REPUBLIC

▲ No more accidents happen in the Bermuda Triangle than in any other part of the ocean. However, because some have not yet been explained, people choose to believe that it is extra-dangerous—and possibly haunted!

100 Some old myths are so powerful that they are used to explain modern ideas. Ancient Greek myths described the Earth as a wise, watchful mother goddess called Gaia. Today, some scientists use Gaia's name for their ideas about ecology. They say that Gaia, the Earth, has powers to heal the damage caused by pollution if only humans would respect her living "body," the natural environment.

QUIZ

1. Have myths and legends now disappeared?
2. What do some people believe flying saucers carry?
3. Where are ships and planes said to disappear?

Answers:
1. No, they still amuse or entertain us 2. Aliens from other planets 3. In the "Bermuda Triangle" area of sea

Index

Entries in **bold** refer to main subject entries. Entries in *italics* refer to illustrations.